Terror in the Library

From outside the room came a low, scraping sound, as if someone were dragging something heavy across the floor. Frozen, Caitlin strained to hear. The dragging sound came closer, then stopped. She didn't dare move, not even to breathe. Was the person who'd scrawled those awful notes crouching outside the door now, this very second? Was he coming to steal another nature project? What would happen when he found Caitlin there?

Scrape. Drag. The doorknob began to turn. Slowly, the door creaked open. Caitlin held her breath. Maybe she was about to solve the mystery of the vanishing creatures. She would discover the identity of the kidnapper! But she might be in terrible danger!

MYSTERY SOLVERS

MYSTERY OF THE

VANISHING CREATURES

MYSTERY SOLVERS

MYSTERY OF THE VANISHING CREATURES

by Gloria Skurzynski & Alane Ferguson

illustrated by Jeffrey Lindberg

Troll

*For Noémi and Dan Mattis
and their grandchildren
Joanna, Aaron, and Cameron*

Text copyright © 1997 by Gloria Skurzynski and Alane Ferguson.
Cover illustration by Jeffrey Lindberg. Copyright © 1997 by Troll Communications L.L.C.

Published by Troll Communications L.L.C.

Printed in the United States of America.

10 9 8 7 6 5 4 3 2 1

CHAPTER

1

"I hate horny toads!" Caitlin Marsh squealed. "Horny toads and snakes and all those slimy things. Get it *away* from me!"

"They're called *horned* toads, not *horny* toads, and they aren't slimy," Joe Daniel Giles said, rolling his eyes. Joe Daniel Giles was in sixth grade, so wriggling creatures didn't bother him. In fact, nothing bothered Joe Daniel. Even though he was only twelve, he could do all sorts of grown-up things. He could rope the horses that lived on his ranch. He could split wood with a real ax. He could even drive his grandfather's ancient rusty tractor. So it wasn't surprising that one little old horned toad didn't bother Joe Daniel at all.

But Caitlin was in third grade, and things like horned toads bothered her plenty. Lily Kato, who was standing next to Caitlin, looked flustered, too.

"Does your horned toad bite, Joe Daniel?" Lily asked in a hushed voice.

"Naw. Lena only bites bugs. I found her sitting in the sand behind our goat pen." He gently stroked Lena's back with his finger. "So I decided to do my nature project on horned toads. I'm telling about how they blend in with the environment so hawks won't eat them."

"I'll bet you'll win first prize," Caitlin told him admiringly. As far as she was concerned, Joe Daniel could do no wrong.

Shrugging, he said, "I don't know about that. It looks like everyone brought great stuff this year."

That was true. The autumn nature fair had lots of entries. The shelves on one whole side of the school library had been cleared so that there'd be plenty of room for the displays. Lily and Caitlin and all the other members of the Three Peaks Elementary School Science Club hoped to go on to the state competition.

Lily had made a poster with different kinds of mountain flowers taped to it. Kevin Running Fox had brought his rock collection. Other Science Club members had created displays of pinecones, fossils, bird feathers, autumn leaves, a wild honeycomb, and even an old, empty wasps' nest.

"Hey, Caitlin," Reese Borden called out, as he set a glass fish tank next to Lily's project. "Want to see what *I* brought?" Reese held out his arm. A brown snake coiled around his wrist like a long spring. The snake's head swayed from side to side, as if it were a tiny windshield wiper, and its thin tongue darted in and out of its mouth like a sewing-machine needle. Reese leaned close to Caitlin. Making a creepy face, he stretched his snake-covered arm toward her.

"Oh, *yuck*!" Caitlin cried.

"This is Fred, my *sssss*nake," Reese hissed into Caitlin's face. "Fred cost a whole bunch of money. I got him from the set of my movie *Snake Bite!* Bet you're too much of a weenie to hold him."

None of the kids in the Science Club liked Reese much, even though he was a movie star. The way he was acting now was a perfect example of why he wasn't very popular.

"Knock it off, Reese," Joe Daniel said. "Caitlin's just scared."

"No, I'm not!" Caitlin really didn't want to touch Fred, but she didn't want Joe Daniel to think she was afraid to handle reptiles, either. She made a quick choice between Fred, the snake, and Lena, the horned toad. "I am *not* a weenie, Reese Borden," Caitlin announced. "Come here, Lena."

Joe Daniel's eyebrows crinkled together, as if he didn't really believe Caitlin. "Wait a minute, are you sure you want to hold Lena? I don't want you to drop her or anything. That floor's a long way down for a toad."

"Don't worry, no-*o-o-o-o* problem," Caitlin said, a little too loudly. She took a step toward the toast-colored creature. Lena just sat there in Joe Daniel's palm, blinking her black, shiny eyes. The spikes on Lena's back looked like pointed tips of meringue on a pie.

Caitlin felt her stomach squeeze. But there was no way she could let Joe Daniel think she was a baby. So she took a deep breath and held out her hand.

Gently, as if the toad were made of spun glass, Joe Daniel set her on Caitlin's open palm. He was right—Lena didn't feel slimy at all. She felt soft and tender, like a baby's skin. She was round and kind of flat, sort of like a hockey puck with a head, a tail, and four legs. Her soft sides puffed in and out as she breathed. Caitlin could feel Lena's small heart beating against her hand.

"See?" Joe Daniel said softly. "I told you it would be okay. Lena's great. You just have to be brave about trying new stuff, Caitlin."

Caitlin managed a small smile. *I can do it!* she told herself. *Now Joe Daniel thinks I'm brave! He might even come over to my trailer after school, and we can sit on the front steps and talk about all kinds of things.*

Caitlin felt pleased with herself until—hop! Lena leaped into the air and sailed to the floor in a toast-colored arc.

"Watch out, Caitlin!" Joe Daniel cried.

"Sorry! I'll get her! Come here, Lena." In a flash, Caitlin had her hands cupped around Lena. But Lena shot between Caitlin's curved fingers and landed two feet away.

Now Joe Daniel's voice sounded impatient. "Move, Caitlin. Let me get her."

"Wait a second!" Caitlin protested. "I can do it." Without waiting for Joe Daniel to reply, Caitlin inched over to Lena so she wouldn't startle her.

From the corner of her eye, Caitlin could see the rest of the Science Club members watching her. She felt a flush of embarrassment. She must look pretty

silly duckwalking across the floor! But she had to catch Lena, or Joe Daniel would think she couldn't do anything right.

Her fingers hovered right over Lena's back. Lena blinked up at Caitlin. She didn't move.

"You're close. Don't scare her," Joe Daniel whispered.

Caitlin's hand closed around Lena. "Got her!" she cried.

The sound of Caitlin's voice seemed to give Lena a fresh jolt of energy. She shot out of Caitlin's hand like a bullet from a gun. In three giant hops, the horned toad was halfway across the floor.

"Keep her away from me!" Lily squealed.

"My snake, Fred, eats toads!" Reese announced happily.

"Get back here, Lena!" Caitlin cried.

Now Lena flopped, hopped, leaped, and jumped in every direction. She landed on Lily's sneaker. "Aaahhh!" Lily screamed, while Joe Daniel shouted, "Everyone, keep still! Don't step on my horned toad!"

The more hands that reached for Lena, the faster Lena seemed to go. Everyone was running, yelling, twisting, reaching, trying to catch the toad that Caitlin had let get away.

Suddenly, the door to the library opened and a boy walked in, followed by the science teacher, Mr. Mahoney.

From her spot on the floor, the first thing Caitlin noticed was the boy's shoes: black leather high-top army boots, laced up tight. The cuffs of worn-out blue jeans were tucked into the high boots. A clean but faded red plaid flannel shirt hung half in and half out of the jeans.

Caitlin's eyes traveled up to the boy's face, the thinnest she'd ever seen on a boy or girl. It was as if his skin had been stretched over his cheekbones. His eyes were as pale as his jeans, and his blond hair was paler still. Caitlin thought he looked like a ghost.

Without a word, the boy crept over to Lena. He moved cautiously, like a wild woodland creature. Gently, he stretched his hand toward the horned toad. A small clucking noise vibrated in his throat, and then—Caitlin could hardly believe it—Lena hopped right onto the strange boy's palm!

"Kids," Mr. Mahoney announced, "I'd like you all to meet a new student at Three Peaks Elementary, and the newest member of the Science Club. Everyone, please welcome Jeremiah Elkins."

"Hi," the other kids said. The new boy didn't answer. Still holding Lena, he stared at the floor. A flush stained his pale cheeks.

"Here, let me take her," Joe Daniel said. "Thanks for catching her."

"Caitlin, why don't you show Jeremiah the nature exhibits?" Mr. Mahoney suggested.

"Come on. I'll show you what's here," Caitlin offered, but the new boy didn't move. He didn't even look up.

What's the matter with this kid? Caitlin wondered.

CHAPTER 2

"Hey, great boots," Reese snickered, pointing at Jeremiah's feet. "Did you just get out of the army?"

Sometimes Caitlin wished she could take a stapler and staple Reese Borden's mouth shut. Especially when it came to saying hello to new kids. Especially with a boy as shy as Jeremiah Elkins.

Jeremiah looked as though someone had slapped him right across his thin face. He colored deep red and ducked his head toward the ground.

Mr. Mahoney stepped forward. "Reese!" he barked. "I need to talk with you in the office! Now!"

"What? What did I say?" Reese asked, hunching his shoulders toward his ears. He smiled a superstar smile at Mr. Mahoney, but Mr. Mahoney just scowled as he opened the door and pointed down the shiny hall.

"No one around here can take a joke," Reese muttered as the door shut behind him.

Darn that Reese! Caitlin thought. *He thinks he's funny, but he can be so mean!*

"Hey, Jeremiah," Joe Daniel began. "You'll have to

ignore Reese. That's what the rest of us do, anyway. So, do you live around here?"

Nothing. Jeremiah didn't even blink. Lily tried to talk to him, too, but Jeremiah stayed as silent as a cement statue, staring at the floor.

Finally Caitlin couldn't stand it another minute. She bent down to about the height of Jeremiah's belt buckle, then twisted to look up into his face. "Hi!" she said, and gave a little wave.

That did it. A smile as slow as maple syrup spread across his face. Without waiting for him to answer, Caitlin reached out and took his hand. It felt as dry as Lena's skin, but not as soft. Jeremiah's palm was rough and chapped.

"Here, I'll show you the exhibits," she told him, pulling him along. "Here are Lily's dried flowers, and Reese's snake."

"Reese," Jeremiah said. Just the one word. Was he asking Caitlin why Reese acted like such a pain? Or did he want to know why Reese, a movie star, went to Three Peaks Elementary?

"Reese . . ." Caitlin didn't know quite what to answer. She didn't like to say mean things about anyone, but with Reese, it was sometimes hard to think of nice things to say. "Reese is . . . well, at least he's not here all the time. Sometimes he's away for lots of weeks making movies. Did you ever see him in a movie?"

Jeremiah shook his head. "I never saw a movie." His voice was so soft, she wasn't sure she'd heard him right.

"You mean you never saw a movie with Reese in it."

Again Jeremiah shook his head. "No. I never saw a movie at all."

"Never at all? How come?"

"My dad . . . he doesn't . . ."

Caitlin waited for him to finish, but Jeremiah clamped his lips shut. Caitlin herself was speechless. How could anyone *never* have seen a movie in his whole life? What kind of strange boy was this?

"So!" she said, trying to fill the silence. "You already saw Lena the Horny Toad—I mean Lena the *Horned* Toad—that's Joe Daniel's exhibit."

"Lena's not a toad," Jeremiah said quietly. "She's a lizard."

"No way. Joe Daniel, Lena's a toad, right?"

But instead of setting Jeremiah straight, Joe Daniel nodded his head. "He's right. They're called toads, but horned toads are really lizards. You got it, Jeremiah."

Wow! Caitlin thought. *This kid doesn't talk much, but when he does . . .* "Here's Chantelle's project," she continued. "It's a box turtle. But I call him a tortoise because . . ."

"He lives on land," Jeremiah finished.

"How did you know that?" Caitlin was surprised. "Hardly anyone knows the difference. The only reason I know is 'cause I looked it up in the encyclopedia."

Jeremiah shrugged, but he smiled a little wider.

"And this," Caitlin said, trying not to sound too proud, "is my exhibit." She pointed to a big Mason jar where six caterpillars crawled along leafy branches. "Those," she said, pausing to let him know how important this was, "will soon spin cocoons. When spring comes, they'll crawl out of their cocoons and be big, beautiful green luna moths." She took a quick glance at Jeremiah to see if he was impressed. He was.

"Luna moths!" he exclaimed, although his voice still wasn't very loud. "They're really rare around here. How'd you get them?"

Caitlin was enjoying this. No one else in the class had been very much interested in Caitlin's wonderful caterpillars. But Jeremiah was staring right at her now, instead of looking at the floor the way he'd been doing.

"This is how it happened," Caitlin told him. "A couple of days before school started, I was outside, in front of the trailer where I live, and there was this huge windstorm. Everything blew around like crazy. So I ran inside, but before I could shut the door, this *huge* green moth blew in. Only I didn't know it was a moth. I thought it was a butterfly."

"Different antennae," Jeremiah muttered.

"The poor thing . . ." Caitlin went on. "Its wings were all torn, I guess from the storm. It couldn't fly—it just kind of flapped around on the floor. So I picked it up and put it in that jar to keep it safe. And the next day . . ."

Jeremiah watched her intently.

"It laid eggs! Inside the jar. But then the moth died." Caitlin felt sad all over again, remembering. "My mother said I could put a pin through the body and mount it on a cork. She said that's what butterfly collectors do. But I just couldn't do that. So I buried it under the lilac bush."

Jeremiah nodded as though he understood.

Caitlin brightened. "Then the eggs hatched into teeny little caterpillars, no bigger than commas on a page."

"They're not so little now," Jeremiah said, sliding his pointer finger along the glass jar. Caitlin noticed how chewed-up his fingernails were. "How'd you know what to feed them?" he asked.

"I didn't, at first," Caitlin answered. "But school started the day after the caterpillars were born, and Chantelle got on the Internet and found someone who knew about things like that. A lepid . . . uh . . . I forget how to say it."

"Lepidopterist," Jeremiah said.

"Yeah. Insect expert. Chantelle's a fifth grader, and she can use computers even better than Mr. Mahoney. This insect lady sent Chantelle some E-mail about luna moth larvae. Baby caterpillars are called 'larvae,'" she explained, in case Jeremiah didn't know, although she was getting the feeling that Jeremiah knew a lot of things. "They eat leaves from walnut trees or beech trees or willow trees."

Jeremiah's eyes skimmed the other exhibits on the shelf. "Whose is that?" He pointed to an ant colony in a rectangular glass cage.

"Oh, that's Mr. Mahoney's. He keeps it here for us to study. And that jar of beetles belongs to Pablo Miramontes. You'll like him—he's always playing jokes on people."

Jeremiah's shoulders seemed to shrink inside his

faded plaid shirt. A frown creased the space between his eyebrows. He began to chew a fingernail.

"Not *mean* jokes! Pablo's not a brat like Reese," Caitlin assured him. But Jeremiah's face had gone stiff.

Speaking carefully, the way she would to a lost puppy, Caitlin asked, "Jeremiah, where did you live before you moved here?"

"Nowhere."

"Nowhere?"

"I didn't move here," he said, looking down as if he were speaking to his shoes. "I've always lived around here. On Bear Claw Mountain."

Puzzled, Caitlin asked, "That's not very far, is it? Why didn't you come to Three Peaks Elementary before?"

"Home schooling," he mumbled.

"Oh." Caitlin knew what that meant. A handful of kids who lived high in the mountains stayed home to be taught, usually by their mothers.

"So what made you come to school now, all of a sudden?" she prodded, since Jeremiah looked as if he wouldn't give out much more information on his own.

"My mother died." He said it so softly that the words didn't sink in at first. When they did, and Caitlin saw how miserable Jeremiah looked, she felt terrible that she'd been so nosy.

"I'm sorry," she said. Just then the bell rang. It was time to go home. Jeremiah turned and ran.

CHAPTER 3

"My turtle must have burrowed way down in his box," Chantelle said to Caitlin. She ran her fingers through the peat moss and leaf litter that made a soft, fragrant home for her pet. "I brought him some grapes to eat, but I can't find him in here."

Chantelle and Caitlin were the only ones in the library this morning. Students weren't usually allowed in school before the bell rang, but the ones with nature fair projects could come early to tend their exhibits. It made Caitlin feel special.

"Come on, Burt. Quit being such a pain!"

Caitlin wasn't paying much attention to Chantelle's fussing. Instead, she stood next to her own luna moth jar, admiring the six brownish cocoons attached to curled leaves inside. Only the day before, the last of her caterpillars had spun itself into its tight winter cocoon.

"Where are you, Burt?" Chantelle kept asking. "Burt Turtle, you've been trying to hide from me all week. Every day I've had to dig you out." Chantelle plunged both hands into the leaf litter and lifted clumps of it at a time. Her voice rose with worry as she said, "He hasn't eaten anything for more than a week. I tried bananas and lettuce and I even dug up some icky worms for him, but he just won't eat. And now I can't find him."

"Want me to help?"

Just as Caitlin reached Burt's box, Chantelle asked, "What is this? A piece of paper," she answered herself. "Buried under the moss. *I* didn't put it there."

"Looks like a note," Caitlin said. "I didn't know turtles could write."

"This is serious, Caitlin," Chantelle snapped, unfolding the paper. As she read it, her eyes grew wide. *"No!"* she cried. "No way! *Burt!"*

Chantelle's fingers pushed through the box frantically as Caitlin picked up the scrap of paper. In big block letters drawn with a black crayon were the words IT WILL NOT LIVE. Caitlin felt her skin prickle with goose bumps.

"I don't believe it! What kind of jerk would steal a turtle?" Chantelle cried as she dumped the box and let the contents spill onto the counter. The two of them stared at the empty pile of peat moss and leaves. There was no doubt about it. Burt was gone.

"Why would anyone . . . ?" Caitlin asked weakly. "I mean, a turtle isn't exactly worth a lot of money."

Now Chantelle's dark eyes flashed. "Burt's worth everything to me! I've had him all summer! He's my pet!"

Caitlin could tell her friend was mad. She tried to

think of something to make her feel better, but her mind was as empty as the pile of litter spread across the counter. Then she got an idea.

"I bet I know who took Burt!" Caitlin declared.

Squinting, Chantelle asked, "Who?"

"Pablo Miramontes. He's always tricking people. I bet he did it for a joke."

"A joke? There's nothing funny about taking Burt!"

"I know. But Pablo thinks everything's funny. I mean, a kidnapped turtle? With a note? It's just Pablo trying to bug you."

The fierce look began to fade from Chantelle's face. "You really think it was Pablo?"

Caitlin nodded hard. "He's probably going to bring Burt back at the Science Club meeting after school today."

"But . . . but what if it's *not* Pablo?"

"Oh, it's Pablo, all right," Caitlin insisted. "It's got to be. Who else would do something like this?"

"I don't know."

"He was probably feeding Burt all along, and that's why Burt wouldn't eat for you." Now that Caitlin had the idea, she was sure she was right. And she didn't want Chantelle to worry any longer.

"Remember when Pablo put Gummi Worms in Mr. Mahoney's ant farm?" Caitlin asked her. "And the time he stuck a comb into a jar of honey and then said he had a real *honeycomb* for his exhibit? And that goofy dance he did when he carried in his beetles—he said he'd caught a famous singing group. Remember?"

A half-smile crept across Chantelle's face. "Yeah, and he *did* put a stuffed skunk in Lily's backpack. I bet you're right, Caitlin. Thanks. I'm glad you were here. But you tell Pablo that if he doesn't bring my Burt with him to the Science Club meeting, *he* will not live. Got that?"

"I'll tell him. Don't worry, Chantelle. Everything will be fine." Caitlin gave Chantelle a thumbs-up. She'd figured out the problem and had helped her friend feel better. There was nothing Caitlin liked to do more than help people. Now she had to find that Pablo!

First she checked the playground, where some of the bigger boys were shooting basketballs, playing H-O-R-S-E. "Anyone seen Pablo?" she asked. She might as well have been talking to the walls. Those boys weren't about to interrupt their game to answer a third-grade girl.

"Have you seen Pablo?" she asked two little girls on the teeter-totter. They shook their heads.

Well, Pablo definitely wasn't in the playground. As Caitlin pushed open the door to go back inside the building, she bumped into Kevin Running Fox coming in the opposite direction.

"Do you know where Pablo is?" she asked him.

"In the cafeteria. He had late lunch today because the teacher made him stay in class and write 'I will not tie peoples' shoelaces together.' Fifty times!"

That Pablo! Always playing jokes. His jokes never

really hurt anyone, but sometimes they could go just a little too far!

In the cafeteria, Caitlin found him sitting at a table, fiddling with the paper wrapper on his straw. When he saw her coming, he blew the wrapper in her direction. It hit her in the stomach.

"Yes!" he cried. "Got ya!"

Shaking her head, Caitlin slid onto the bench and scooted right next to him.

"Look, Pablo, I've got to talk to you. You know Chantelle's turtle?" Caitlin began.

"I've seen him, but I wouldn't exactly call him a friend," Pablo answered. He laughed at his own joke. Then he picked up a chicken nugget and shoved it into his mouth.

"Don't be dumb. Listen, I already figured out that it was you. It's not funny, Pablo. Chantelle's really upset. You've got to give Burt back. She said to tell you if you don't bring him to the meeting, you're dead. And she means it."

Pablo stopped chewing. He stared right at Caitlin. "What are you talking about?"

"Chantelle's turtle. He's gone. You took him and left a nasty note in his box."

"Wait a minute." Pablo looked suddenly serious. "I didn't take anybody's turtle. I wouldn't do that. No-*o-o-o* way."

From the look on Pablo's face, Caitlin knew he was telling the truth. With a sinking feeling she realized she'd picked the wrong suspect.

Pablo's eyebrows drew together so they almost touched in the middle. "Wait a minute. Did you tell Chantelle I stole Burt?"

Caitlin nodded.

"So that's why she's been mad at me all day. Thanks a lot, Caitlin!"

"Well, you're always playing tricks on people and . . . I was only trying to help . . ."

Pablo jumped out of his seat and grabbed his tray. "First of all, my jokes aren't mean. Whoever stole Burt is really rotten. And second of all, you shouldn't go accusing people before you check. I *didn't* do it. Thanks to you, whoever stole Burt has had even more time to get away!" He looked up at the large clock that hung on the lunchroom wall. "There's only ten minutes until recess is over, and I've got to find Chantelle and tell her someone else kidnapped her turtle."

"I'm sorry—"

But Pablo was already gone.

Caitlin worried the rest of the day, right up until the last school bell rang. Now she'd have to face all the Science Club members. Everyone would know that she'd goofed again. They would probably tell her she needed to think before she talked. It made her stomach hurt to count how many people might be mad at her. She thought about missing the meeting, but if she wanted to win at the nature fair, she'd have to show up to take care of her luna moth cocoons.

Her hands were cold and sweaty as she turned the knob on the library door. Inside, all the Science Club members stood gathered around Chantelle's empty box. They were staring, whispering, shaking their heads.

"Who would do something like this?" they murmured.

"Look at those notes. What do they mean?"

Just then, Pablo glanced up and saw Caitlin.

Caitlin took a deep breath. She knew she'd have to apologize again to Pablo. But before she had the chance to open her mouth, Lily ran over and took her hand. "Oh, Caitlin, I'm so sorry," she said.

"I'm the one who's sorry," Caitlin answered. "I know I'm always saying things I shouldn't—"

"We all feel really bad about—" Kevin broke in.

"I know. I never should have told Chantelle that Pablo—"

"We feel bad about Chantelle and you, too," Lily interrupted. "Your luna moths are gone."

"My moths? *My cocoons!* They're *gone?*"

Hurrying across the room, Chantelle put her hand on Caitlin's shoulder. "It's true. They were stolen, just like Burt. All we found was this note." She pressed a piece of paper into Caitlin's hand. With trembling fingers, Caitlin opened the ragged note.

Inside, in heavy black letters, were the words THEY WILL BE MONSTERS!

CHAPTER
4

"**S**omebody stole my caterpillars!" Caitlin wailed. "I raised them from babies! We have to call the police!"

Lily placed her thin arms around Caitlin and gave her a hug. Caitlin couldn't help it—even with the rest of the Science Club watching, hot tears rolled down her cheeks. She didn't care if Joe Daniel thought she was a baby. She'd raised those tiny wiggling creatures to the cocoon stage, and now someone had walked into the library and taken what was hers. But who? And why?

"Whoever stole my cocoons should go to jail!" Caitlin cried.

"Hey, don't look at me—I didn't do it!" Pablo insisted. "I can see why someone would take a turtle, but who the heck would want a bunch of bugs?"

"*I* want them!" Caitlin declared. "They're special."

Pablo snapped his fingers. "I got it! Whoever stole your cocoons needs them for turtle food!" He started to laugh, but Lily and Chantelle whirled on him.

"You're not even funny, Pablo Miramontes," Chantelle shouted. "Caitlin loved those luna moths."

Lily's dark eyes flashed. "How would you feel if someone ate *your* project?"

"You mean my beetles?" Pablo asked, still grinning. "Beetles are good—especially medium rare."

When the three girls glared at him, Pablo's smile melted from his face. "Come on, guys! I was only kidding." He swallowed hard and said, "I—I'm sorry for what I said, Caitlin. About the turtle food thing."

"It's okay," she answered. She meant it, too. If they were going to catch the thief, it was important for the Science Club members to put their differences aside and work together.

Just then the door opened and Jeremiah slipped inside. He looked like he was about to say hello until everyone started to talk all at once.

"Jeremiah, guess what? Somebody came in the library and stole Caitlin's luna moth cocoons—"

"And left weird notes—"

"We're going to call the sheriff—"

"And they'll throw the thief in jail for a hundred years!" Caitlin finished.

Speaking so low that Caitlin wasn't even sure she heard it, Jeremiah said, "You're going to call the police?" His pale face seemed to go even whiter. "Are they going to come here? To Three Peaks Elementary?"

"We're not going to call the police. Everybody just calm down for a second!" The voice belonged to Joe Daniel. He began to pace back and forth. He seemed to be trying to get things straight in his mind. "First of all, does anybody know where Mr. Mahoney is?"

"I saw him at the office," Jeremiah told him. "He said . . . he said to start the meeting without him."

"All right. Let's just sit at a table and try to figure this out. We're going to need paper and pencils."

As if by magic, everyone quieted down and took seats around the library table. Notebooks flipped open, pencils appeared. Jeremiah slipped in beside Caitlin on one side, and Lily sat at her other side. Caitlin couldn't help but notice how nervous Jeremiah seemed as he fumbled around trying to find his notebook. Finally, Caitlin gave him a sheet of paper and one of her extra pencils.

"Thanks," he said softly.

"Okay," Joe Daniel began. "Let's try to think this through one step at a time. It's the only way to figure things out. Write down WHAT, WHO, and WHY. We'll start with the easiest. What."

"A turtle and a jar of luna moth cocoons," Chantelle said.

"Okay. So what's next?" Pablo asked.

"Who? Who did it?" Caitlin shouted, at the same time Joe Daniel said, "Why. We need to know why before we can guess who. Let's examine the evidence. Chantelle, hold up your note."

Chantelle read out the crayoned words on her note, "It will not live." Her lips trembled.

Caitlin was already holding up her note. "They will be monsters," she read aloud. "How could

31

anybody write that my moths would be monsters?" Caitlin asked. "Luna moths are just about the most beautiful creatures in the world, all green with pretty yellow dots on their wings."

"Okay, Caitlin, we believe you. What kind of paper are the notes written on?" Joe Daniel asked.

"Just a piece of notebook paper," Caitlin answered. "The same kind I have. The same kind everyone has."

"And with black crayon," Lily added. "Probably to make it look spooky."

"Red would have been scarier," Pablo said. "Like *blood*."

"Shut up, Pablo!" the girls yelled at him. "You're getting as bad as Reese."

"Yeah, Reese," Kevin said. "Where *is* Reese?"

Lily shrugged her shoulders. "I saw him earlier today, and then he just . . . disappeared."

"Yeah," Chantelle said. "He was here this morning, but he wasn't around the rest of the day. I wonder what he's doing?"

Reese, Caitlin thought to herself. *Reese is gone, and so are my moth cocoons. And Chantelle's turtle.* Suddenly it all became clear to Caitlin. It was like finding just the right piece to a puzzle. It all fit perfectly.

"Everybody," she said loudly, "wait! Listen to me! I think I know who took our stuff." She stood up, so that she could see everyone around the table. All their eyes were focused on her.

Caitlin took a breath and blew it out between her teeth. "I used logic, just like Joe Daniel said to do, and

I think I have the answer. I think the person who took our projects is someone in the Science Club."

"You mean, you think it's one of us?" Kevin Running Fox cried. "No way!"

There were a lot of murmurs of "I don't think so," and "Uh-uh, I don't believe it."

But Caitlin knew she was right. She had to be. She locked her hands across her chest and went on.

"Look, whoever took Burt had to get him out of school, right? So it's someone who goes to Three Peaks, right? Someone we wouldn't notice."

"Maybe . . ." Pablo said.

"Okay. So, which one of us left school early today?"

"Well . . . Reese," Chantelle answered.

"Right!" Caitlin exclaimed. "And who was here this morning, giving him lots of time to kidnap Burt and my cocoons before he sneaked away?"

"Reese," Lily said.

"And who's the only person who didn't come to this meeting? Reese Borden!" Caitlin cried.

"Oh, come *on!*" Pablo snorted. "Reese could buy a hundred turtles and a thousand moths. Just because he isn't in school doesn't make him guilty."

Joe Daniel shook his head slowly from side to side. "I'm with Pablo. I can't see Reese stealing. Besides, you haven't answered the other part of the question. Why. Why would he do something like that?"

"Because—maybe Reese was afraid if Burt or my moth cocoons were in the nature fair, his snake wouldn't win. And Reese *always* has to win."

Now everyone sat in silence. Caitlin knew they had to think this over, hard. Caitlin sank back down into her seat. Maybe, when she grew up, she would be a detective. She liked the way she figured out a problem before anyone else. Joe Daniel would have to notice that she could think as fast as a sixth grader. . . .

The door opened, and Mr. Mahoney stepped inside. "Sorry I'm late," he said. His gold wire-rimmed glasses had slid down his nose, and he pushed them up with his finger. Today, Mr. Mahoney had on a pair of jeans and a blue denim shirt. Caitlin always liked the way her teacher dressed, almost as if he could walk out of the school and right into a forest. "Well, it's great to see you all at work." Mr. Mahoney smiled at them. "What are you guys up to?"

"We're trying to figure out who stole Chantelle's turtle and Caitlin's cocoons," Pablo began. "Caitlin says it's Reese, but I'm not so sure."

"Oh, no. Caitlin, are your luna moth cocoons gone, too?" the teacher asked.

Caitlin nodded. "There was another note."

"That's terrible. But what makes you think Reese Borden took your cocoons?"

Suddenly, there seemed to be a bunch of crickets jumping around in Caitlin's stomach. Now that her teacher was staring at her, she wasn't so sure of her idea. "Well," she began weakly, "Reese was in school this morning, and then he was gone."

"Yes, that's right," Mr. Mahoney said.

Caitlin swallowed. It was harder explaining her

theory with her teacher's eyes boring into hers. "So I figured he took our stuff and then left school to hide them. See, I thought maybe he wanted to win a prize at the nature fair. . . ."

"Caitlin, Reese has been filming a commercial for the ski lodge. His mother picked him up at school this morning. I don't think he could have smuggled a turtle and a jar of moth cocoons out of school with his mother watching."

"Oh," was all Caitlin could think to say.

"See?" Pablo muttered under his breath. "I told you, Caitlin."

"It's good that you're trying to think things through, Caitlin, and I'm sure you were only trying to help, but the thief isn't Reese. Someone *else* is taking your projects," Mr. Mahoney declared.

Wrong again. She'd been so sure, and she'd been wrong. Even worse, her cocoons were still gone, and she wasn't any closer to solving the mystery.

CHAPTER 5

"**H**ey, is anybody in here?" Caitlin asked as she poked her head through the library door. Silence. "Hello!" she called out. When there was still no answer, she felt herself grin. Yes! She had the whole library to herself, which meant she could study all the nature exhibits for clues.

Every Thursday Caitlin's mom made the long drive to town to mail a stack of ski hats that she'd knitted. The money she made by selling them was used to support herself and Caitlin. Then she'd swing by Three Peaks Elementary to pick up Caitlin and Joe Daniel. Even though Caitlin sometimes had to wait an extra few minutes for her mother to arrive, she loved the time alone in the library. She would pretend that every brightly colored book on the shelves belonged to her.

She breathed deeply, enjoying the smell of books and slick-paper posters, pencil shavings and glue. Enjoying the soft silence that she could almost feel . . .

But wait a minute! From outside the room came a low, scraping sound, as if someone were dragging something heavy across the floor. Frozen, Caitlin

strained to hear. The dragging sound came closer, then stopped. She didn't dare move, not even to breathe. Was the person who'd scrawled those awful notes yesterday crouching outside the door now, this very second? Was he coming to steal another nature project? What would happen when he found Caitlin there?

Scrape. Drag. The doorknob began to turn. Slowly, the door creaked open. Caitlin held her breath. Maybe she was about to solve the mystery of the vanishing creatures. She would discover the identity of the kidnapper! But she might be in terrible danger!

The door opened farther. A foot appeared—a sixth-grade-sized foot, in a worn sneaker.

"Joe Daniel!" Caitlin screamed. "What are you doing? You scared me to death!"

"Huh?" Joe Daniel looked surprised. "Why should you be scared? I'm just dragging in this box, that's all. It's full of petrified wood for the exhibit. It's very heavy."

Caitlin collapsed against the table. "I thought maybe you were Thump-Drag!" she panted.

"Huh?" Joe Daniel said again. "Who the heck is Thump-Drag?"

Caitlin could feel her eyes go wide. "Don't you know anything? Thump-Drag!"

Joe Daniel stared at her blankly.

"The guy who had his arms and legs cut off when he was in a horrible accident while he was on a camping trip."

"Thump-Drag *camps*?" Joe Daniel asked.

"Yeah. It's true! For revenge, Thump-Drag goes to all the tents, dragging himself on his chopped-off arms. It sounds like this. *Thump . . . dr-aaa-g. Thump . . . dr-aaa-g.*"

Joe Daniel just stared at Caitlin. "That has got to be the *stupidest* thing I've ever heard."

"Uh-uh," Caitlin said. "I heard about it on a Girl Scouts' camping trip."

But she could feel her ears burn. Maybe Joe Daniel was right. Maybe it was just a made-up story that Girl Scouts told around campfires to scare one another. Now Joe Daniel would think she was an idiot for believing it.

"I can't stand around listening to stupid junk like that," Joe Daniel said. "I have to feed Lena. She hasn't been eating right lately, so I got her some mealworms at the feed store." He opened a paper bag and took out a plastic container shaped like a margarine tub. "She ought to like these."

"Can I watch you feed her?" Caitlin asked.

"I don't care."

An I-don't-care was as good as a yes, so Caitlin crowded next to Joe Daniel as he lifted the screen that covered Lena's cage. She heard Joe Daniel gasp. His knuckles went white where they leaned against the library shelf.

"What's wrong?" Caitlin cried. She stared into the empty cage, searching for the horned toad. She hoped Lena had just burrowed into the sand. But instead of seeing a toad-shaped bump underneath a layer of sand, Caitlin noticed a piece of notebook paper. It lay next to the tipped-over water dish.

With shaking hands, Joe Daniel picked up the scrap of paper and unfolded it. Written in black crayon were the words IT WILL DIE.

He stared at the note for a whole minute before he turned to Caitlin, his voice harsh. "Whoever took Lena is going to be sorry. I'm gonna find him. I swear I will."

Caitlin had never seen Joe Daniel look so fierce. His face was pale except for red splotches on his cheeks. His lips were pressed together tightly. Then they parted, as he read the words out loud. "It . . . will . . . die! That *jerk!*"

"We have to go now," Caitlin said, almost afraid to speak because Joe Daniel was so angry. "My mother will be waiting outside."

On the ride home, Joe Daniel sat slumped in a corner of the backseat, not talking. Caitlin felt almost as sorry for his loss as she did for her own. In fact, she felt sorry for all three of them—Joe Daniel, Chantelle, and herself. Their projects meant a lot more to them than just exhibits for the autumn nature fair. They were living, loved pets! And now they were gone.

The drive home seemed to take much longer than usual, maybe because most of the trees had lost their autumn leaves and looked drab and dejected. Or maybe because Joe Daniel was so silent.

"Is that the new boy from your club?" Caitlin's mother asked suddenly from the front seat.

"Where?" Caitlin peered through the car window. "Yeah, I think it's Jeremiah. He must have missed the bus."

To get a better look, she rubbed a clean spot on the side window. It was Jeremiah, all right, in his too-big brown parka, with his backpack slung over his right shoulder and his books clutched in his left hand.

"Maybe he'd like a lift." Caitlin's mother stopped the car right next to Jeremiah, who turned toward them in surprise. "Roll down the window, Caitlin, and ask him," Mrs. Marsh said.

"Hi, Jeremiah," Caitlin called through the opened window. "Did you miss the bus?"

He just stared at them.

"We'll give you a ride," Caitlin said, opening the door. "There's room back here, right, Joe Daniel?"

"I guess," Joe Daniel muttered, still gloomy.

Jeremiah shifted his books from his left hand to his right. He shuffled his feet in the dry, fallen leaves at the side of the road. "I—I—" he stammered. "Thanks but . . . I'll walk."

"Okay. He wants to walk, Mom."

Caitlin's mother drove forward, leaving Jeremiah behind. "What an odd boy," she commented.

"Yeah, he's kind of weird, but he's okay," Joe Daniel answered.

Caitlin twisted around to stare out the back window. Jeremiah was still standing there at the side

42

of the road, watching them drive away, his backpack on his shoulder, his books in his arms.

Caitlin turned back and clutched Joe Daniel's hand, hard. "He's the one," she murmured, too shocked at what she'd just realized to even shout. "I'm positive. Jeremiah's the one who took Burt and my cocoons and Lena."

"Sure, Caitlin," Joe Daniel scoffed. "Just like you knew it was Pablo. Then you were positive it was Reese. Now, it's Jeremiah. Next, you'll probably say I did it. Get real, Caitlin."

She sank back against the car seat. It didn't matter if Joe Daniel believed her or not. Caitlin knew she was right!

CHAPTER
6

"Caitlin, I have to get started right away on the next batch of ski hats," her mother said. "I fixed some tuna salad sandwiches. They're in the fridge. Just eat whenever you're hungry, and I'll eat later."

"Okay, Mom." Caitlin was already hungry, even though it was only four o'clock in the afternoon. She peered into the refrigerator. Half a dozen tuna sandwiches sat on the shelf, each wrapped in a plastic bag with a tucked-in top. Caitlin took two.

Her mother was already concentrating on the knitting machine, threading different colors of yarn to start making one of the brightly colored ski hats. Each hat had a name woven into it—Tricia or Mark or Paul; Ramon or Raquel or any of hundreds of other names. Making those hats paid the rent for April Marsh and her daughter Caitlin, put gas into their old car, and provided tuna sandwiches and all the other meals they ate, week after week.

"Mom, I'm going to eat outside," Caitlin told her.

"Mmm-hmmm," her mother murmured. "Put a coat on. It's getting chilly. Halloween isn't far away."

"I know." Caitlin shrugged into her old green parka. It was too small for her, but good enough to wear around the trailer court. Right now, near the end of October, hardly anyone lived in the trailer court anyway, except Caitlin and her mother and their neighbor, Mrs. Chesnut. In two more months, though, the other trailers would start filling up as ski instructors, lift operators, and ski-resort workers rented them for the winter season.

While she sat on the steps chewing her sandwiches, Caitlin looked around to find the biggest pile of autumn leaves. She loved to jump on leaves, scuff through them, or kick them into the air. Autumn leaves felt so crunchy. And they smelled good—like the earth.

"Yahoooo!" she yelled, flinging a handful of dry leaves into the air. They fell on her like a shower of pennies—copper, rust, and mustard-colored. She was making so much noise that she didn't hear the clop of horse's hooves until they practically reached her.

"What are you doing?" Joe Daniel asked.

Feeling silly, Caitlin peered up at him. Up there, seated so high on his horse, Joe Daniel looked really tall.

"Nothing," she answered. She picked bits of leaves out of her hair and off her parka. "Nothing at all. I was just . . ."

Joe Daniel didn't listen to her answer. He swung out of the saddle and stood in front of her, holding

Holly's reins. Holly was his own special horse, his golden palomino.

"I've been thinking," Joe Daniel told her, "about what you said in the car. I think . . . maybe you were right."

"What? Really? What part did you think I was right about? All of it, or just a little bit?" If Joe Daniel thought she'd been right about something, Caitlin wanted to know exactly what it was.

"The whole thing," Joe Daniel answered. "The part where you said Jeremiah was the one who took our exhibits—"

"Because Jeremiah had such a long way to go and he still wanted to walk instead of ride the bus or get in the car with us," Caitlin broke in. "I *knew* he wouldn't do that unless—"

"Unless he had something to hide. Like Lena."

"You want to know how I figured it out?" Caitlin's voice rose to a squeak. "It was the books. He was carrying a big stack of books, right?"

"Yeah."

"Books are heavy. When we drove away, I was thinking about how hard it would be to carry those all the way home. Then I saw his *backpack*," Caitlin said. "That's when I knew. No way would Jeremiah haul a bunch of books clear to Bear Claw Mountain in his arms. Not when he had a backpack he could carry them in."

"Right," Joe Daniel finished. "Unless he had Lena in his backpack, and he didn't want the books to squash her."

46

Caitlin nodded and tried to keep a smile from splitting her face in two. When she'd said all those things, Joe Daniel had told her she was crazy. Now he'd changed his mind and he agreed with her!

"I've got to get Lena back before something happens to her," Joe Daniel went on. "I'm going to ride up the mountain to where Jeremiah lives. So . . . do you want to come with me?"

"H-how?" Caitlin stammered.

"On Holly. She can carry both of us. You'll ride behind me."

Before he'd finished speaking, Caitlin jerked open the door to her trailer and yelled, "Mom, I'm going for a ride with Joe Daniel on Holly."

"Did you eat your dinner?" her mother called back.

"Yes!"

"Okay. Be home before dark."

Caitlin hesitated. It was already about four-thirty. On these days in late October, darkness started to gather around five-thirty. That didn't leave much time to ride all the way to Bear Claw Mountain. Caitlin squeezed her eyes and considered. She didn't want to miss a chance to be with Joe Daniel. And it wouldn't be really, truly, all-the-way-black, can't-see-your-hand-in-front-of-your-face darkness until well after six o'clock. They might be back by then.

"I will, Mom," she shouted.

Then Joe Daniel was boosting her up into Holly's saddle. Caitlin grunted, and her too-tight parka almost popped its zipper when she stretched her leg across Holly's broad back. Holly snorted as though she wasn't sure she wanted Caitlin to be there. But when Joe Daniel swung smoothly onto the saddle in front of Caitlin, Holly quieted down. He made a clicking sound with his teeth, and they started out.

Caitlin had to hold tight to the saddle when Holly broke into a trot. Puffs of dust rose up from the horse's hooves. Although the sun had turned deep red, it seemed as if no time at all had passed before they reached the base of Bear Claw Mountain.

The wind blew hard. With one hand, Caitlin pulled her parka's hood closer around her ears. That made it harder to hear Joe Daniel when he said, "I just don't know why Jeremiah would do it. I thought he was an okay guy. If he had Lena in that backpack, she better be okay, or I'll . . ."

He didn't finish saying what he'd do if anything bad happened to Lena.

They followed the dirt road that climbed through pinyon pines and stunted juniper trees. Those trees stayed green all year, but here and there a scrub oak glowed dull orange, or a maple's last few leaves blazed red. And the aspen trees! The quaking aspens twirled their small gold leaves like jewelry spinning on thin chains. Even when the leaves dropped from the branches, they spun all the way to the ground.

As the road grew steeper, Caitlin leaned forward to keep her balance on Holly's back. Holly had stopped trotting; now she moved at a brisk walk.

"I asked Jeremiah what part of the mountain he lives on," Joe Daniel was saying. "We ought to be getting pretty close. I think we turn off the road right about . . . here!"

Joe Daniel turned the horse onto a tire-rutted side road. Caitlin had to grab him to keep from sliding sideways. "Sorry," she mumbled.

"'S'okay. Keep a lookout for a cabin, or smoke from a chimney, so we can tell if we're getting close. I don't want to just go up and knock on the door. I want to look around first."

The sun had dropped behind the peak of Bear Claw Mountain now, leaving the woods in shadow. Branches rustled.

"Is that the wind?" Caitlin asked nervously.

"Maybe it's a black bear," Joe Daniel said, "eating so he'll get fat before he hibernates. A bear needs plenty of body fat to last him through the winter, you know."

The horse whinnied. "Yep, Holly smells some animal or other, for sure," Joe Daniel declared.

"What's that?" Caitlin exclaimed. "Over there!"

"Maybe it's a great, big, ferocious grizzly! Why do you think they call this Bear Claw Mountain?" She could tell Joe Daniel was teasing her.

"No. I mean, over there," she said. "It's some kind of a shed, or a barn, or something. Maybe that's where Jeremiah hid Lena and my cocoons and Burt the Turtle."

"I doubt it, but I'll go have a look." Joe Daniel slid

down from the saddle. "You stay here with Holly, Caitlin."

"No way! If there's a bear around, I'm coming with you." Awkwardly, Caitlin stuck her foot into the stirrup and lowered herself to the ground, which seemed a long way down.

"Well, okay, but we'll have to tie up Holly." Joe Daniel wrapped the reins loosely around a tree branch and said something softly to his horse. Then he whispered, "Come on, Caitlin, and don't make any noise."

It was hard *not* to make noise. Since there was no path leading to the shed, leaves and branches crackled beneath their feet. "How are we going to see inside when we get there?" Caitlin whispered. "It'll be dark." The dusk had faded so much that she strained to tell what was real and what was shadow.

"I brought a flashlight," Joe Daniel said, as if it were the most natural thing in the world to carry a flashlight in his coat pocket. He pulled it out and switched it on.

The door to the shed hung crookedly, partway open. Joe Daniel stopped right in the opening and swept his flashlight beam around the inside. "Oh, my gosh!" he exclaimed.

"*What? What?*" Caitlin bumped against his back. He wouldn't move, and she couldn't see anything because he was taller than she was.

"They really are here!"

"What? My cocoons? Let me see!"

"Everything," he said.

And there they were. On a splintery shelf stood Caitlin's jar of luna moth cocoons. Beside it was a dusty glass aquarium filled with moss and leaves and covered by a screen. From behind the scratched glass, Lena's black eyes shone in the flashlight beam. And Chantelle's turtle moved his front feet, trying to dig a passage down into the peat moss.

"Are they alive? Are they hurt? Are they okay?" The words tumbled from Caitlin. "Burt and Lena look all right, don't they, Joe Daniel? And my cocoons are still hanging from the branch in the jar, just like they were before they disappeared."

"So he *did* take them," Joe Daniel said, shining the flashlight on one creature after another. "And he didn't hurt them. But why did he take them? I still don't understand."

Suddenly the door to the shed creaked open. "Hey!" a deep, rough voice shouted. "Who's in there? What are you doing?"

Joe Daniel whirled and pointed the flashlight at the doorway. It blazed on a man in a heavy wool coat. The man had a thick black beard. Wild, matted hair stuck out from under his peaked cap. His big hands curled around the barrel of a shotgun. And the gun was pointed right at Caitlin and Joe Daniel!

CHAPTER 7

"**G**et that light out of my eyes," the big man barked, "and get out here where I can see you."

Except for the flashlight beam, the shed was dark. Caitlin stood stock still. What should they do? Obey? Or make a run for it?

"Now!" the man roared, batting at the light shining in his eyes with one hand, as if it were a pesky fly. The other hand held the shotgun steady.

"Okay!" Joe Daniel turned off the flashlight and reached for Caitlin's hand. The two of them moved cautiously toward the huge, threatening silhouette.

"Get outside here," the man ordered them. A full moon had just risen over the mountain, making enough light for them to see one another. The man squinted at them. "Wait a minute," he said. "You're just a couple of kids." Caitlin felt a flood of relief as the man lowered the gun barrel so it was pointing at the ground.

"What are you two doin' up here, anyway? You tryin' to steal somethin'?"

"No!" Joe Daniel said. "We're friends of Jeremiah Elkins."

"That's a lie!" the man bellowed. "Jeremiah doesn't have any friends."

That made Caitlin mad. "Sure he does! He has lots of friends. I know he's kind of quiet and he could use a good haircut, but everybody likes him anyway," she declared. "Well, at least, we all did until he took our nature exhibits. But nobody knows about that yet, except Joe Daniel and me—"

"Shut up, Caitlin!" Joe Daniel muttered, his voice tense.

Caitlin went on talking anyway. "You must not know Jeremiah Elkins," she told the man, "because if you did, you'd know he has *lots* of friends at school."

The big man startled them by laughing out loud. "Oh, I think I know Jeremiah Elkins," he said. "He's my son. So I'm goin' to ask you two one more time. What are you doin' out here in my shed?"

Caitlin was about to tell him, but Joe Daniel grabbed her arm to silence her. "We came to talk to Jeremiah about our school projects," he said quickly. "We went into your shed because that's where he's keeping our stuff."

"What . . . ?" Caitlin began, but Joe Daniel squeezed her arm harder as he added, "There's a turtle and a horned toad and a jar of cocoons. Go in and check if you want."

"That's okay," Jeremiah's father said. "I already seen 'em. That kid of mine's always foolin' with some darned creature or other. Well then, seems we gave each other a scare for nothin'. I'll get Jeremiah and send him out to you." Mr. Elkins turned and tramped away from them, his heavy boots scattering the fallen leaves like dust.

When the man was out of earshot, Joe Daniel turned and hissed, "Caitlin, you're always shooting off your mouth! If you told Mr. Elkins about our exhibits being stolen, you might have gotten Jeremiah into big trouble. His father looks mean."

At that moment, the back door of the cabin burst open. Jeremiah ran toward them, the tails of his plaid shirt flapping. When he reached them, he stopped suddenly and stood in front of them, panting a little. "Hi. My—my dad says you want to see me," he stammered.

Joe Daniel didn't waste any time. He didn't even say hello. "Why did you take our projects?" he demanded.

"You put them in your shed," Caitlin accused him. "They're going to freeze to death out there."

"But . . . but they *have* to be outside," Jeremiah answered, hurrying after Joe Daniel and Caitlin as they returned to the shed. "I wasn't trying to be mean. I was trying to save them—"

"Save them? By stealing them?" Joe Daniel cried, shaking his head. "I don't think so. If they get sick because you left them in the cold . . ." Joe Daniel took an angry step toward Jeremiah. "Look," he said in a low voice. "You stole them, and I want them back!"

"No! Listen to me!" Jeremiah raked his fingers through his ragged hair. His voice was louder than Caitlin had ever heard it. "All of them—the horned toad, the turtle, and the cocoons—they have to be cold this time of year."

"Cold? Why?" Joe Daniel asked.

"Because Burt and Lena are animals that hibernate. That's why Chantelle couldn't get Burt to eat," Jeremiah said. "His nature told him it was time to hibernate, so he quit eating and tried to dig a burrow."

"So?" Caitlin said.

"So animals that hibernate use all their fat to live on while they sleep." Jeremiah's forehead wrinkled with the effort to explain. "When they're out in the wild, they dig into the ground to hibernate. It's cold, so their hearts start to go real slow, and everything in their bodies kind of shuts down. The thing is, hibernation can't work unless the animal stays cool. Don't you get it? They can't hibernate in a warm room. They'll die!"

"They'll *die*?" Joe Daniel asked. Caitlin could tell he was trying to understand, just like she was.

"If Burt and Lena had stayed in the library, they would have hibernated, but their bodies would have stayed warm, just like the room. So their hearts would have kept beating fast. And with their hearts pumping like that, all the fat—their stored food—would burn up. None of the fat would be left, and they'd get weaker and weaker. But they'd still be sound asleep." Jeremiah crossed his arms over his chest. His voice was suddenly strong. "I'm telling you that if Burt and Lena had stayed in that library, by spring they would have starved to death."

Caitlin frowned. Jeremiah's words were beginning to make sense.

"Even if you're right about Burt and Lena, why did

you take my cocoons?" she asked.

"Because they need to be outside in the cold weather so they don't develop too fast," Jeremiah explained. "Moths aren't supposed to come out of their cocoons until spring. In a warm room, they'd come out of their cocoons in the middle of winter, and they'd be all undeveloped and weird. Like monsters."

Neither Joe Daniel nor Caitlin knew what to say.

"I was only trying to keep them alive," Jeremiah pleaded.

Quietly, Caitlin asked him, "Why didn't you just tell us?"

Jeremiah looked down at the floor. He made a half circle with his boot in the dust. "I . . . I usually don't talk like I think. It's kind of hard for me, especially when I'm . . . the only one who's new. I stayed after school and saw how sick Burt looked. So I just left a note. I was going to tell you guys, but everyone started talking about calling the police. I just got . . . scared," he said.

Joe Daniel smiled a little. "You're talking pretty good right now, Jeremiah."

Jeremiah said, "That's because I'm talking about animals. I'm never scared when I'm talking about animals."

The three children walked out into the moonlight just as the back door to the cabin flew open once again. Mr. Elkins was standing in the doorway. "Jeremiah, come in here!" he yelled. "And bring those two kids with you."

"Uh-oh," Caitlin muttered. "Your dad sounds mad."

"He's not mad. He always sounds that way. He's just loud," Jeremiah assured them. "My dad's okay."

They followed him into the small cabin, where the smells from a woodstove made Caitlin's mouth water. On a rough, wooden table, Mr. Elkins had spread a red-checked tablecloth, wrinkled as if it had been folded inside a drawer for a long time. A bowl of shiny apples sat in the center, next to three mugs of hot chocolate.

"Thought you might like this," Mr. Elkins said, taking a pan of cornbread out of the oven. "We got strawberry jam, too. You kids dig in, now," he told them. "Then we'll telephone your folks to let them know where you are. They might be worried—it's pretty dark outside."

"Thank you so much," Caitlin said with feeling. Not just because of the food, which looked wonderful. A phone call might keep her out of trouble, since she'd promised her mother she'd be home before dark.

As Caitlin stared around the small, crowded cabin, she noticed books everywhere—on the chairs, on the shelves, even on the floor. Most of the books were about animals and nature. Jeremiah's books.

"How'd you two get here?" Mr. Elkins asked.

"On my horse," Joe Daniel answered.

"Well, then, Jeremiah and I will saddle up and ride with you down the mountain. Just so's you don't lose your way. Want some marshmallows in your hot chocolate?"

"Yes!" all three kids shouted at once. Then they laughed. Even Mr. Elkins had to smile.

CHAPTER

8

"**N**o. I don't want to go in there," Jeremiah said, pulling back. "I don't want to tell them what I did."

"They already know," Caitlin said. "You *have* to face them sometime. Come *on!*"

"No—"

Just then, Mr. Mahoney opened the door to the library and motioned them inside. "Caitlin, Jeremiah, come in," Mr. Mahoney told them. "We've been waiting for you. Now our special meeting can get started. We've got a lot of things to talk about today."

The whole Science Club had gathered in the library. Kevin, Chantelle, Pablo, and Joe Daniel sat on one side of the table, while Reese and Lily sat on the other. Mr. Mahoney pointed to two empty seats next to Lily and said, "Why don't you two sit down?"

"Um . . . okay," Jeremiah muttered.

"Hey, Jeremiah, I heard about what you did!" Reese called out. "So you're the one who took the critters. And you wrote scary notes and everything." Pounding his fist onto the tabletop, Reese said, "I hate it when I have to film commercials. I always miss the good stuff at school!"

Caitlin could feel Jeremiah shrink back toward the door. Clamping her hand on his arm, she pulled him in the direction of the table. "It's okay," she whispered.

But Jeremiah looked like a kitten facing a pack of dogs. He crammed his hands so deeply into his pockets, it seemed as if his pants had swallowed his arms. Caitlin led him to the empty seat next to Lily and sat down beside him. Mr. Mahoney cleared his throat.

"Well, Jeremiah, I've heard quite a story from Caitlin and Joe Daniel. I'm ashamed to admit that even though I'm your teacher, I couldn't figure out the connection between the turtle, the cocoons, and the horned toad. But you did. You're a real scientist."

"His dad says he's always taking care of creatures," Caitlin volunteered. "Jeremiah knows *everything* about animals. And he was just so worried, but he didn't know how to tell us and—"

"Yes, I'm sure you're right." With his finger, Mr. Mahoney pushed his glasses back up his nose. "You know, Jeremiah, because you understood science so well, all those animals will be alive next spring. Everyone in this room is grateful to you."

Even though Jeremiah's head was bowed, Caitlin could see a tiny smile flicker across his face. His hands, which had been balled into fists, relaxed.

But then Mr. Mahoney crossed his arms over his chest. "The problem is that even though your reason for doing what you did was good, you still took things that didn't belong to you. And I'm afraid I can't just let that go."

The tiny smile disappeared from Jeremiah's face.

"So if everyone agrees," Mr. Mahoney said sternly, "my idea is to have Jeremiah create a new exhibit for the nature fair. A panorama on hibernation."

"Hey, that would be *great!*" Caitlin squealed.

"Yeah!" Joe Daniel grinned. "No one knows more about hibernation than Jeremiah."

Chantelle nodded and gave Jeremiah a thumbs-up. "It'll be a cool project," she said. "And thanks for saving my turtle. I owe you one."

"Yeah, welcome to the club," Pablo said.

"Just don't ever scare me like that again," Lily added. "Those notes were too creepy."

Jeremiah ran a hand through his hair so that it stood up in blond spikes. "I . . . I don't know what to say."

"I always know what to say," Reese broke in. "I'm an actor. It's my job. And what I want to say is that my mom's making me get rid of Freddie the snake, just because she found him in our toilet. Is that fair?"

All the girls said, "*Oooooooooh!*"

"So Fred needs a new home," Reese told Jeremiah. "Will you take him? I trust you with him."

"Sure, I'll take him," Jeremiah said.

"I've got him right here in my backpack," Reese said, unzipping the red nylon case. "Here, Caitlin, hand Fred to Jeremiah for me."

Reese put the snake right under Caitlin's nose.

Caitlin took a deep breath. She'd held Lena—could Fred be much worse? "Okay," she answered, letting out her breath in a big puff as she reached for the snake.

Before she could touch Fred, Jeremiah leaned forward and took him from Reese. "He shouldn't be handled by too many people," Jeremiah said. "I know you really want to hold him, Caitlin, but maybe some other time."

Jeremiah smiled at her in his shy way. *He's so easy to like*, Caitlin thought.

"Well, that's it, then," Mr. Mahoney said. "Meeting's over. Let's get to work on the nature fair."